"Memories are the best thing in life,
I think."

Text copyright © 2020 by Amir Nada
Illustration copyright © 2020 Rezdewi Studio
ISBN: 978-0-6489288-0-5

On the beautiful island of Bali, just a short scamper from the warm sea and the dazzling white sand, lived a small brown rat. He had twinkly eyes and long, twitchy whiskers. His name was Miró.

Every morning, Miró met up with his friends, Budi and Wayan. Budi and Wayan had brown and grey fur and long tails as Miró did, but they were much bigger than him. Miró sometimes wished he were a little bigger.

The three rats liked to sit on the beach, but they were careful to keep out of the way of all the humans. They warmed themselves in the sunshine while they decided what to do that afternoon.

Sometimes they visited the temple. It was a long run from their beach, and tiring in the heat, especially for little Miró. He often had to stop for a rest, and to gulp down a refreshing drink of puddle water.

On other days they went to the rice paddies, where they sat for hours, fishing on their wooden boat. They never caught a thing, not even a beetle, but it didn't matter because the rice was just as delicious.

After each long and tiring day, the three
friends crept into the hotel by their beach.
They stole little bits of fish and crusts of
bread from under the nose of the hotel chef.

Full from their feasting, the rats headed to the beach, where they sat in a row to watch the sun go down over the sea. "This is the best bit of the day," squeaked Miró.

Budi and Wayan laughed at him. "Aren't you forgetting something?" Wayan asked. 'There's something we could do that's MUCH more fun. Come on, let's go." Miró took one last look at the sunset and trotted after his friends.

The three rats slunk along by the hotel. But they didn't go inside. Instead they found a bedroom window to tap on with their scratchy claws. Tap, tap, tap they went until they woke a sleeping child.

As soon as the child opened the curtains, Budi, Wayan and Miró pulled the very scariest, nasty, ugly faces you can imagine, their eyes gleaming evil yellow in the moonlight. How terrifying they looked!

As the little boy screamed, the three rats ran away. Budi and Wayan squealed with laughter. Scaring children was their favourite thing to do. Miró felt bad about it, but he joined in with their laugher anyway, just to fit in.

They found another window. A young girl was staring looking out of it. The rats immediately began to pull faces, doing their best to scare her. But the girl didn't seem scared. She stood quite still and stared back at the rats.

The little girl's name was Charlie. 'That's odd,' she said to herself. There was something different about the smallest rat. What was it? "Oh, poor little thing. You're not scary, you just look sad!"

Charlie reached her hand out towards the window. The three friends jumped back, startled, and shot away into the dark. They'd done enough scaring for one night. It was time to go to home to their beds.

Charlie was sorry to see Miró leave.
But the following night the rats came
back. This time, Charlie laughed when
they pulled their scary faces. Miró
found himself laughing along with her

Charlie had a great idea. She would follow the rats and see where they lived. She saw Budi and Wayan run up to their home, where their family was waiting. 'Dinner's ready,' said their mum, and Budi and Wayan rushed inside, licking their lips.

"Bye," called Miró to his friends as he trotted further along the path, with Charlie behind him. Miró came to an old palm leaf near a rubbish bin, and crept underneath. There was not another rat to be seen.

"You poor thing," Charlie whispered to herself. "You don't have a family. That's why you look so unhappy." Charlie decided she should help Miró, but she didn't know how to. Deep in thought, she trotted back to her hotel.

"The next day started as it always did for the three rats. But, after a long, hot trek to the temple, they were ravenous, and raced back to the hotel eager for all the scraps they could find."

Way ahead of Miró, Wayan and Budi tore along the passage and turned into the kitchen. But then they skidded to a halt, frozen in terror. In front of them was an enormous, ferocious CAT!

They turned and fled, running for their lives.
"Quick," said Wayan, "this way!" All three scooted
out of reach of the cat, inside a covered drain.
Shaking with fear, they stopped to get their
breath back.

"It's awful being so scared," said Miró, thinking of all the poor children they'd frightened. "Yes," agreed Wayan and Budi. They hid in the drain until the cat left, then slunk home, felling guilty for all their bad deeds.

The following morning, Miró waited on the beach for his friends. He waited and waited. They didn't come. Puzzled and hurt, Miró walked along to their home, but when he got there, their nest was empty. They'd gone!

BEWARE
CAT
GONEAWAY

Miró didn't know what to do without Wayan and Budi. He hid under his palm leaf all day until sunset. He was so hungry. Then he thought about the little girl. She had looked kind. Perhaps she would help him.

Charlie was waiting when Miró tapped at her window. She let him in, gave him some scraps to eat, and cuddled him. 'Some people might think you're a dirty rat, but I know you are friendly and sweet,' she said.

Charlie's plan worked. At the end of the holiday, she hid Miró in her rucksack and took him back home. Her parents were a bit cross at first, but not for long. As for Miró, with Charlie's care, he grew to be strong, healthy, and happy.

Made in the USA
Monee, IL
17 December 2020